Baby Brightly Shining   by Joshua Klein

Brightly Shining
The Horse That Nobody Wanted

by Joanne Beusch

Printed in the United States of America

First Printing, 2015

ISBN 978-0-9970671-0-1

Published by

Joanne M. Beusch
Baltimore, Maryland

jbeusch@msn.com

Young Brightly Shining   by Julia Klein

This book is dedicated to the entire Brightly Shining Team which has made her the competitor she is today. It is based on the true story of a beautiful off track thoroughbred headed for an unknown future and the person who saw her potential as a hunter in the show ring.

I would also like to thank Julia and Joshua Klein for their inspiration and their contribution of artwork in the completion of this book.

Valentine's Day on the farm.

It was Valentine's Day and everyone on the farm was very excited as they stopped by to see the pretty little chestnut filly born earlier that morning. She had three white stockings and a large blaze on her face. As she stood on her four wobbly legs, the sunlight was streaming through the barn door and made her chestnut color shine a bright red. Her mother named her Brightly Shining.

She quietly settled into life beside her mother. She learned to play and get along with the rest of the horses on the farm. She was having a lot of fun running through fields and eating grass in her pasture, but Brightly Shining knew that it would not be long before she would have to leave her mother and begin training to become a racehorse like her father and grandfather.

Brightly Shining never came close to winning a race.

Brightly Shinings' mother tried to prepare her for life as a racehorse. It would be very different from her life on the farm and a lot harder.

It did not take long for her to realize just how difficult being a racehorse would be. She tried her best to run very fast but the other horses would always catch her. She was always the last horse, or the next to last horse, to reach the finish line. She never came close to winning a race and she knew she would never be good at it.

Brightly Shining knew that she was a disappointment to her family of proud thoroughbred racehorses.

Brightly Shining spent most of her time in her stall crying.

Scared and afraid of what was going to happen to her, Brightly Shining was taken to a nearby farm where she would have a new job. She was hoping that someone at her new home would teach her something that she would be able to do well. Unfortunately for Brightly Shining this was not going to happen. She spent most of her time in her stall crying and wishing she could go back on the farm with her mother. Then early one morning before her usual breakfast of grain, she was led onto a trailer and shipped to a cold, noisy place.

Brightly Shining was not sure where she was.

Brightly Shining was not sure where she was, but she knew she was cold, nervous and scared. As she paced back and forth in her stall, strangers watched her through the door. She heard someone say, "We can't do anything with this one she will never make a good horse for anyone." She heard another person say, "Nobody is going to buy this one." Poor Brightly Shining, as she stood alone in her stall she thought, "If nobody wants me, what is going to happen to me."

The older man told her "you are coming home with me."

Suddenly, while she was facing the back of her stall she heard a click and then the stall door opened. As she turned around she saw an older man with a kind face staring at her. She heard him say, "Come here girl." She walked over to him and put her head down. The two people with him told him that he would never be able to train a wild horse like her. He closed the stall door and walked away. Brightly Shining started pacing again, faster than before. A few minutes later she heard her stall door open again. The same older man was standing there. This time he was alone. She again walked over and put her head down. This time she heard him say, "You are going to be alright girl. You are coming home with me. I am going to teach you to be a show horse."

It was dark and cold when Brightly Shining arrived at the barn that would be her new home. The older man carefully took her off his trailer and led her to a stall in his barn. He kept telling her that she was going to be okay and she hoped he was right.

Brightly Shining's new home.

The next morning was sunny and warm for a November day when the older man and one of his students came to the barn. Brightly Shining soon learned his name was Mr. Mike and his student was Annie. Mr. Mike asked Annie to brush her and give her a bath. Brightly Shining thought that she looked so pretty after Annie scrubbed her three white stockings and her face.

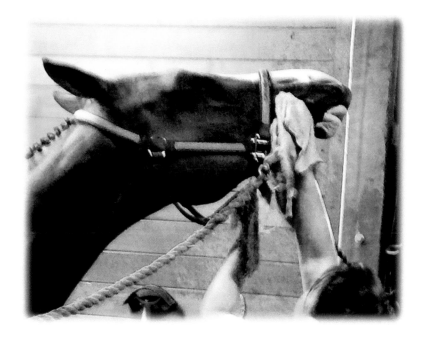

Bath time!

After a few days Mr. Mike decided it was time to start Brightly Shining's training program. He talked to her and told her he was going to teach her how to jump, how to hold her head and how to act like a show horse. She was very excited at the thought of learning something new.

Mr. Mike talked to Brightly Shining.

Under Mr. Mike's watchful eye, Annie put a saddle on Brightly Shining to ride her in the training ring. They rode around in circles for a while and then they decided to jump a log in the middle of the ring. Together they went flying over the log with no effort. Brightly Shining thought "This is fun, maybe I can learn to do something that I can do really well."

As Brightly Shining continued to train, she could tell that Mr. Mike was very pleased with her. He kept telling her how well she was doing, but he reminded her that she had to "practice, practice, practice"!

Brightly Shining and Annie went flying over the log.

As Brightly Shining settled into her new home she became friends with the other horses on the farm who had special names like hers. There was Happy Cowgirl, Heart's Desire, Spectacular Eve and Outwit. She especially enjoyed talking to Outwit.

Brightly Shining enjoyed talking to Outwit.

Brightly Shining also liked Mr. Mike's dog Rocky who would sit by her stall door and bark at her. She thought that Rocky was a funny little dog.

Rocky and Brightly Shining.

Brightly Shinings' first horse show.

Since Brightly Shining was doing so well, Mr. Mike decided it was time to see how she would do in the show ring. As she prepared for her very first horse show her mane and tail were braided and her white stockings and face were shining. She jumped and trotted and walked just like Mr. Mike had told her to do. She and Annie did very well and even won a few ribbons.

Mr. Mike took Brightly Shining and Annie to a lot of different places to compete against a lot of very good horses. They continued to win ribbons of all colors. Brightly Shining celebrated her first year at Mr. Mike's farm with all of her new friends. She was so happy with all that she had learned and she thought her mother would be very proud of all that she had accomplished.

As the weather got colder, it was time to develop a plan for the following year. Because Annie and Brightly Shining had done so well during their first year in the show ring together, Mr. Mike decided that it was time to go to some of the bigger competitions where they would ride against some of the best horses in the country. Mr. Mike could see that Brightly Shining was not too sure about this plan so he told her that the only thing he wanted was that she do her best. He told her that they may win some classes but they would also lose classes; he wanted her to be a good sport no matter what happened.

Brightly Shining and Annie had done well during their first year together.

The day finally came for her first big competition. Mr. Mike cleaned his best saddle and bridle and Annie wore her best show clothes. Brightly Shining was so proud of the way she looked but she was very nervous. As Annie guided her into the show ring she forgot everything she was supposed to do. She hopped over jumps like a kangaroo and could not remember a thing Mr. Mike told her to do. She was so upset with herself and she saw the disappointment on everyone's face after only one class when they led her back onto the trailer for the ride home.

Ready for her first big competition!

On the way home she noticed that Mr. Mike drove right past his farm. She started to worry that she really was the horse that nobody wanted, not even Mr. Mike or Annie.

Mr. Mike drove right past his farm.

When the trailer stopped Brightly Shining noticed a lot of other horses all dressed to show and she wondered where she was. Mr. Mike took her off the trailer and Annie was right there with him. He told her he had entered her in more classes. She did not have time to be nervous or even think about what she was doing. She did very well that day and was so happy that Mr. Mike and Annie still believed in her.

Brightly Shining studied the course for her class.

Brightly Shining smiling in the show ring.

Brightly Shining got better and better the more she practiced and competed. People began to notice her and commented that she seemed to smile as she competed. She was always ready to pose for pictures with her ribbons no matter what color they were. She loved the pink ones as much as she did the blue ones. She realized that she enjoyed what she was doing and had worked hard to become very good at it.

Brightly Shining knew once and for all that she would no longer be the horse that nobody wanted!